CORAL REEF HIDEAWAY

The Story of a Clown Anemonefish

SMITHSONIAN OCEANIC COLLECTION

Book copyright © 2005 Trudy Corporation and the Smithsonian Institution, Washington, DC 20560.

Published by Soundprints, an imprint of Trudy Corporation, Norwalk, Connecticut.

Book Design: Shields & Partners, Westport, CT

First Paperback Edition 2005
10 9 8 7 6 5 4 3
Printed in Indonesia

Acknowledgments:
     Soundprints would like to thank Dr. Victor Springer of the Department of Vertebrate Zoology at the Smithsonian's
National Museum of Natural History for his curatorial review.
     The author thanks the following individuals for their input and expertise: Dr. Daphne Fautin of the University of
Kansas, Dr. Terry Goslinger of the California Academy of Sciences, Dr. Joel Elliott of Queens University, Ontario,
and Dr. Gerald Allen of the Western Australia Museum.
     The illustrator wishes to thank Peg Siebert, Children's Librarian at Blodgett Memorial Library, for her invaluable
assistance in researching and reference for this project, the entire staff at Blodgett Memorial Library for their support,
Dana M. Rau for her professional, thoughtful oversight of this project, my family for their patience and Bud and
Evelyne Johnson for their guidance and support.

ISBN 1-59249-480-3 (pbk.)

The Library of Congress Cataloging-in-Publication Data below applies only to the hardcover edition of this book.

Library of Congress Cataloging-in-Publication Data

Boyle, Doe.

Coral reef hideaway : the story of a clown anemonefish / by Doe Boyle ; illustrated by Steven James Petruccio.
     p.   cm.
Summary: A clown anemonefish, that lives in the delicate tentacles of a sea anemone, finds a mate, lays her eggs,
and protects them from other coral reef animals until they hatch.
     ISBN 1-56899-182-7
1. Clown anemonefish—Juvenile fiction. [1. Clown anemonefish—Fiction. 2. Fishes—Fiction.
3. Coral reef animals—Fiction.]
I. Petruccio, Steven, ill. II. Title.
     PZ10.4.B67Co 1995   95-6776
     [E] – dc20   CIP
                                               AC

CORAL REEF HIDEAWAY
The Story of a Clown Anemonefish

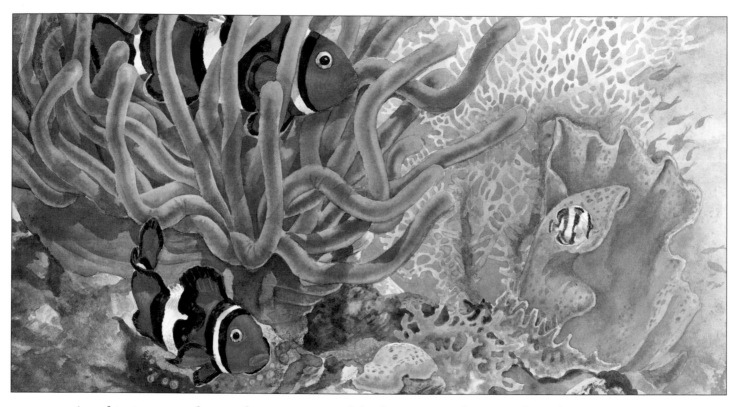

*Amphiprion percula, or clown anemonefish, live among the tentacles of sea anemones,
underwater flower-like animals imbedded in the sand or attached to rocks or coral.*

by Doe Boyle   Illustrated by Steven James Petruccio

Soundprints®
Where Children Discover...

It is dawn near Papua New Guinea, the western Pacific island north of Australia. The first rays of the sun strike the lagoon, and the barrier reef beneath the surface floods with light. The clown anemonefish, Percula, gently stirs the delicate tentacles of her sea anemone home.

Living in the shelter of its twisting arms, Percula is unharmed by the stinging cells on each tentacle. She is protected by a slimy coating that covers her from mouth to tail.

Her enemies would not so easily escape the sting of the anemone. Percula is safe in her hideaway.

Tiny sea animals drifting on the ocean current catch on the swaying tentacles. Percula nibbles at them briefly, then wanders away to graze on the fine green algae that grows on a nearby coral.

A pair of butterflyfish race by Percula. They too are protected from the anemone's darts. With Percula gone, the fish rush to eat her anemone's tender purple tips.

Fiercely, Percula charges the butterflyfish. With a swish of their fins, they escape her attack.

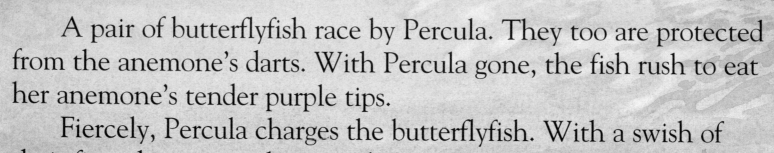

Soon the reef is filled with brilliant midday sunlight.
Colorful pairs of angelfish and clouds of yellow damselfish
feed among corals, sea fans and feather stars.

A small male clown anemonefish comes to Percula's
hideout, looking for a home. Percula needs a mate, so
she allows him to stay.

One day Percula's mate begins to prepare a nest. Choosing a rock tucked at the anemone's base, he clears away algae and grit with his mouth.

He is not the only creature cleaning today. Close by, a coral grouper hangs motionless near an elephant-ear sponge. Small fish called cleaner wrasses swim around him. They feed on his dead skin and tiny crustaceans attached to his scales. Like dentists, the wrasses also clean his teeth and gills.

Percula's mate must be careful. He watches the wrasses while he cleans the rock. If they get the chance, some wrasses will eat the anemonefish eggs when they are laid.

Before twilight the rock is clean. Percula's mate rests near the anemone mouth as darkness falls. Now, sharks, jacks and barracudas swarm around the shadowy reef, snapping up blue tangs and parrotfish who have stayed too long in their daytime waters. Percula and her mate are safe in the anemone.

As the nearly full moon rises over the lagoon, the reef's night creatures emerge. Like thousands of miniature stars, the coral itself blooms. Squirrelfish and soldierfish leave the sheltered crevices and hunt along the bottom for worms and crabs.

In the moonlight, Percula's mate swims rapidly up and down like a horse on a carousel. He chases and nips at Percula.

Just before morning, Percula moves to the clean rock beside her anemone. Swimming slowly in a zigzag pattern, Percula brushes her belly across the rock's surface, leaving behind hundreds of glistening orange-red eggs. Percula's mate swims behind her, fertilizing the eggs as they are laid.

For five days Percula's mate closely guards
the nest, chasing away the egg-stealing wrasses.
He fans the nest with his fins, providing
oxygen-rich water to the eggs.

On the morning of the sixth day, Percula awakens to the sound of rainfall. The nearby island is lush and green because of the rains, but today the rain pelts too hard. The island's rivers overflow their banks. Mud fills the rushing water.

Percula hurries to her mate as the rain drums the sea above her. She needs to help him guard their precious eggs.

The rain continues. The muddy rivers race down the mountainside. Soon the water of the reef is blurred with fine brown silt. The silt can choke the coral and kill Percula's eggs.

Percula and her mate frantically fan their eggs and keep them clean. They pluck away bits of plants swept along by the murky water.

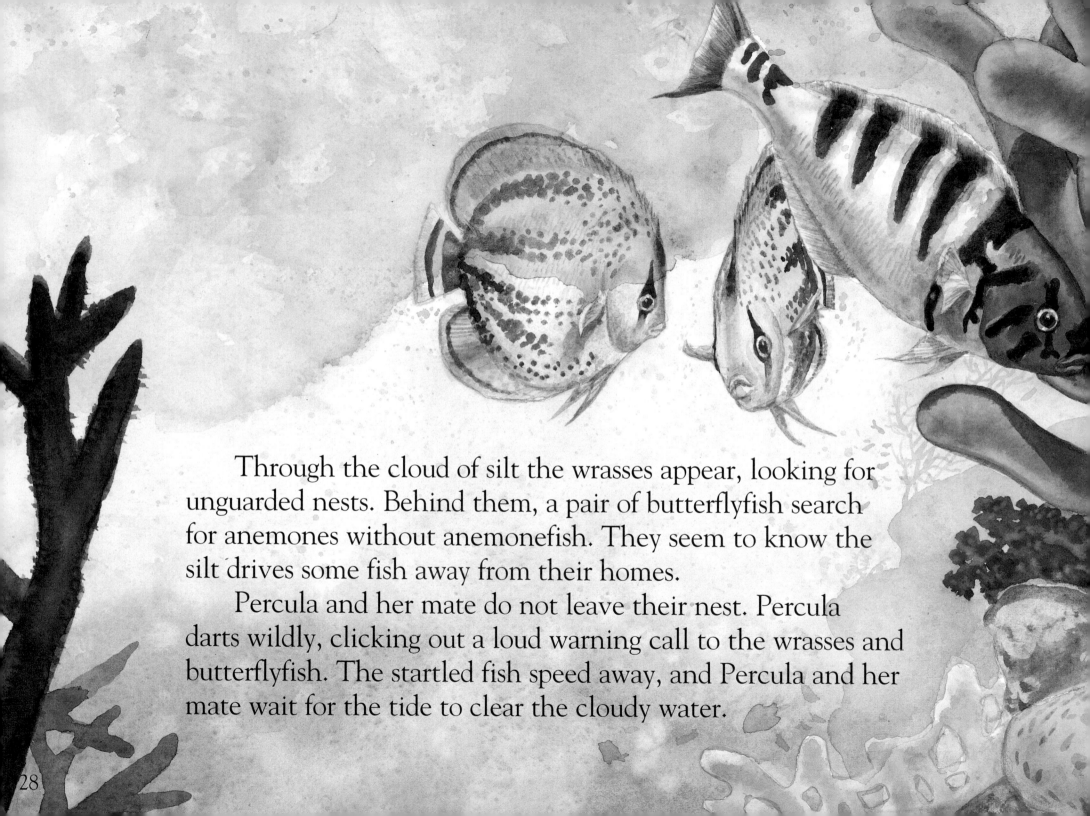

Through the cloud of silt the wrasses appear, looking for unguarded nests. Behind them, a pair of butterflyfish search for anemones without anemonefish. They seem to know the silt drives some fish away from their homes.

Percula and her mate do not leave their nest. Percula darts wildly, clicking out a loud warning call to the wrasses and butterflyfish. The startled fish speed away, and Percula and her mate wait for the tide to clear the cloudy water.

After dark on the seventh day, Percula's eggs hatch. Tiny and transparent, the baby anemonefish rise toward the moonlight. Riding the ocean current, they feast on plankton. Soon they leave their parents far behind.

Percula and her mate rest. The anemone wraps its gentle tentacles around them, and the moon pulls the tide quietly over the coral.

About the Clown Anemonefish

The clown anemonefish is a small tropical fish, 2 to 3 inches long, that lives in the warm shallow waters of the Indian and Pacific oceans. It is called an anemonefish because it lives in close connection with sea anemones—tubular, flower-like sea animals that have tentacles with stinging cells. Sea anemones are imbedded in the ocean floor or attached to other firm objects, such as rocks. The clown anemonefish, commonly called clownfish, is nicknamed "Percula" in this story because its scientific name is *Amphiprion percula*. It is one of twenty-eight species of anemonefish that live in close association with the ten species of sea anemones that cause it no harm.

Both the anemonefish and their host anemones are part of the wonderfully diverse habitat of the coral reef. Though threatened by pollution and human interference, the coral reefs teem with life.

The behaviors described in this story are typical of both the clown anemonefish and other anemonefish. Scientists are continuing to discover new facts about anemonefish in studies done both in aquariums and in the oceans. The exact reasons that anemonefish are able to live in harmony with the anemones without getting stung are still unknown, but evidence indicates that the relationship benefits both animals.

Glossary

barrier reef: A ridge of coral built up from the ocean floor parallel to the coastline and separated from the shore by an area of shallow water.

crustaceans: Aquatic animals with hard shells and segmented appendages, such as lobsters, crabs and barnacles.

gills: The structures on the sides of a fish's head, hidden by a cover called an operculum, that take oxygen from the water so that the fish can breathe.

lagoon: A shallow area of water partly separated from the ocean by a narrow strip of land or barrier reef.

plankton: Tiny sea plants and animals that drift in ocean currents.

silt: Very fine, loose particles of sand or soil that are carried by flowing water.

tentacles: Flexible body parts of certain saltwater animals that are used like arms or fingers to catch prey.

wrasse: A small, slender, often brilliantly colored or silvery fish that lives in warm seas.

Points of Interest in this Book

pp. 4-5, 8-9: plate coral (flat greenish).
pp. 4-5, 8-9, 14-19, 26-27: encrusting coral colony (aqua).
pp. 4-5, 8-9, 16-17, 28-29: staghorn coral (spiky dark).
pp. 4-9, 12-15, 22-25, 28-29: sponges (pinkish dotted).
pp. 4-9, 12-15, 18-27, 30-31: fire coral (lime green).
pp. 4-5, 8-9, 18-19, 24-25, 26-27: sea whips (long thin).
pp. 8-9, 20-21, 24-25: brain coral (rounded green).
pp. 8-11, 14-17: sea fan (yellow tree-like).
pp. 8-11, 16-17, 20-21: soft coral (branch-like red-orange).

pp. 10-11, 14-17, 22-23: elephant-ear sponge (bright orange).
pp. 10-11, 14-15, 24-25, 28-29: butterflyfish.
pp. 12-13: feather star, yellow damselfish, angelfish (striped).
pp. 14-15: coral grouper (red), cleaner wrasses (sleek, long).
pp. 16-17: tube sponge (tubular yellow), barracuda (long thin gray), bar jacks (gray), gray reef sharks, blue tang (blue), parrotfish (colorful).
pp. 18-19: squirrelfish.
pp. 22-23, 28-29: six-banded wrasses.